Wind

A Level One Reader

By Alice K. Flanagan

The
Child's World®

Listen to the wind.

See how it blows.

Wind is moving air.

6

The sun makes air move.

The warm air rises.

The cool air flows down.

Strong winds can bring bad storms.

Strong winds can also
blow clouds away.
Then the day might
be sunny again.

Wind can blow away
soil. It can even wear
away rock.

Wind spreads seeds that grow into new plants.

Wind can help us travel across water or through the air.

What else can wind do?

Word List

air

blows

moving

seeds

soil

spreads

storms

wind

Note to Parents and Educators

Welcome to Wonder Books®! These books provide text at three different levels for beginning readers to practice and strengthen their reading skills. Additionally, the use of nonfiction text provides readers the valuable opportunity to *read to learn*, not just to learn to read.

These leveled readers allow children to choose books at their level of reading confidence and performance. Nonfiction Level One books offer beginning readers simple language, word choice, and sentence structure as well as a word list. Nonfiction Level Two books feature slightly more difficult vocabulary, longer sentences, and longer total text. In the back of each Nonfiction Level Two book are an index and a list of books and Web sites for finding out more information. Nonfiction Level Three books continue to extend word choice and length of text. In the back of each Nonfiction Level Three book are a glossary, an index, and a list of books and Web sites for further research.

State and national standards in reading and language arts emphasize using nonfiction at all levels of reading development. Wonder Books® fill the historical void in nonfiction material for the primary grade readers with the additional benefit of a leveled text.

About the Author

Alice K. Flanagan taught elementary school for ten years. Now she writes for children and teachers. She has been writing for more than twenty years. Some of her books include biographies, phonics books, holiday books, and information books about careers, animals, and weather. Alice K. Flanagan lives with her husband in Chicago, Illinois.

Published by The Child's World®
P.O. Box 326
Chanhassen, MN 55317-0326
800-599-READ
www.childsworld.com

Photo Credits
© Clarissa Leahy/Tony Stone: 5
© CORBIS: 2
© Craig Lovell/CORBIS: 18
© Digital Vision/Getty Images: 10
© EyeWire/Getty Images: 9, 13
© Jean L. Batt/Taxi: 17
© Karen H. Mason/CORBIS: cover
© Kevin Schafer/CORBIS: 21
© Michael Kornafel/Tony Stone: 6
© Peter Lillie/Gallo Images/CORBIS: 14

Editorial Directions, Inc.: E. Russell Primm and Emily J. Dolbear, Editors;
Alice K. Flanagan, Photo Research; Emily J. Dolbear, Photo Selector

The Child's World®: Mary Berendes, Publishing Director

Library of Congress Cataloging-in-Publication Data
Flanagan, Alice K.
  Wind / by Alice K. Flanagan.
     p. cm. — (Wonder books)
Summary: Simple text describes the wind, how it is formed, and its
effects on the world.
Includes bibliographical references and index.
  ISBN 1-56766-455-5 (lib. bdg. : alk. paper)
1. Winds—Juvenile literature. [1. Winds.] I. Title.
II. Series: Wonder books (Chanhassen, Minn.)
  QC931.4 .F55 2003
  551.51'8—dc21
                              2002151614